DESERT RESCUE

Timothy Peters

Also by Timothy Peters

The Josh Powers Series:
Jungle Rescue
Alaskan Rescue
Rescue From Camp Wildwood
The Rescue of Josh Powers

DESERT RESCUE

TIMOTHY PETERS

ABUNDANT HARVEST
PUBLISHING

Formatting: Erik V. Sahakian
Cover Design/Layout/Photo: Andrew Enos

All Scripture is taken from the New King James
Version of the Bible. Copyright © 1979, 1980, 1982 by
Thomas Nelson, Inc. Used by permission. All rights
reserved.

Library of Congress Control Number: 2019937868

ISBN 978-1-7327173-5-0
Second Printing: September 2019

FOR INFORMATION CONTACT:

Abundant Harvest Publishing
35145 Oak Glen Rd
Yucaipa, CA 92399
www.abundantharvestpublishing.com

Printed in the United States of America

TABLE OF CONTENTS

CHAPTER 1...9

CHAPTER 2...20

CHAPTER 3...31

CHAPTER 4...39

CHAPTER 5...47

CHAPTER 6...58

CHAPTER 7...68

CHAPTER 8...75

CHAPTER 9...84

CHAPTER 10...94

Thank you to Jeremiah Peters for technical support, Erik Sahakian for formatting, and to my wife, Shawn, for allowing me the time to write.

*For my grandchildren, Brooke and Vance Grimm,
and Benaiah, Guinevere, and Amos Peters.*

Chapter 1

Josh Powers cruised along in his bright blue and white Piper PA-11, only 150 feet above the ground. His dad told him he'd need to fly through the restricted area below two-hundred feet. When rounding the mountain and over the white lake-bed, the plane glided effortlessly in the still, calm air—almost like sliding on glass.

It's a great day for flying.

Soon, when he flew over Nevada's Emerson Lake, he was finally able to fly at the altitude he wanted.

The airport he had to find was somewhere on the other side of the lake. But the blinding sun reflecting off the alkali made it hard to see. He flew on for ten minutes with no change of scenery. All he could see was the flat, barren, waterless lake-bed.

Josh passed over a black pickup truck with a camper shell. The hood and the driver's door were open. But he didn't see anyone.

Then, as he flew over a short red flag, Josh spotted the runway. "There it is." This runway was the same color as its surroundings. The only thing that made it stand out, were the four small red flags marking each corner. At the other end of the runway, a windsock and wooden bench—where people could wait for their plane ride—came into view.

Must be the waiting area at Emerson International Airport, Josh thought.

As he got closer, Josh caught a glimpse of a man lying face down on the ground behind the bench. Papers flew haphazardly out of an open suitcase—clothes were scattered.

"Oh man, I hope that's not Mr. Geesler." Josh stepped down on the left rudder. He turned the plane around to better see the body. It didn't look good.

He radioed for help. "This is Piper 2-3 Juliet-Papa, 2-3 Juliet-Papa. This is Piper 2-3 Juliet-Papa. There's a man down on the runway of Emerson Dry Lake. Do you read me? Over." Josh repeated this five times but no one replied. He switched to another channel and tried again.

This time a military pilot answered him. "2-3 Juliet-Papa. Roger ... I will ... it ... Over."

Josh heard nothing but a buzzing sound through his earphones.

It had been a few months since he rescued his father from the notorious drug dealer, Carlos Martinez, in El Salvador. Josh had flown right into the midst of the trouble and got himself caught by the same dangerous drug cartel. Geesler, however, was supposed to be a simple pick-up. Josh shoved his adventures in the jungle to the back of his mind.

The bright blue and white Piper, the PA-11 Josh was flying now, was one of his favorites. The Piper PA-11 had one seat for the pilot and one seat in the back for a passenger. Both had controls. His father gave it to him after the rescue in the jungle.

"This would be a great first airplane for a young pilot," his dad had said.

He continued to fly in a circle, looking for anyone who might help the man who lay lifeless on the ground. With no rescue in sight, he flew to the end of the runway. Checking the windsock, he turned his little airplane into the wind and pulled back on the throttle. The airplane began its slow descent. And as it came slowly to the ground, Josh pulled back on the stick to stall the plane inches from the ground.

He taxied toward the bench and stopped short, afraid the prop-wash would scatter the man's papers even more.

"Here goes." Out of the airplane he crawled, looking around to make sure he was safe.

The sweltering sun stung his skin. Sweat trickled down his neck. The smell of the dry, alkali desert made him thirsty.

"You better take some water along." It was the last thing his father told him before he left. Josh laughed out loud. His father was one to always make sure you took care of yourself as well as the job, which had to be done.

Cautiously, Josh walked toward the body on the ground; still not sure if it was Mr. Geesler. Goosebumps covered his body as he scanned the horizon.

He knelt down, and with trembling hands turned the man over. A large lump was on the side of the head. Dried blood covered half the face. "Mr. Geesler? Mr. Geesler, is that you?"

No response. No movement either. "Oh, please don't be dead." Slowly Josh reached out and placed his hand on the chest feeling for any sign of life. He checked for a pulse on the man's neck. Suddenly, the body twitched. Josh heard a moan. He jumped back. But then, for two or three long minutes the bloodied man lay still. Finally, another moan and he struggled to sit up.

"You better lie still, mister."

"Where ... my notes ... where are they?" The old man mumbled.

Josh ran to the airplane for the canteen of water and raced back.

"Where are my papers? Where is my suit-case?"

"Let's wipe some of the blood off your face," Josh said.

"Where are my papers?"

Josh took out his handkerchief and poured some water on it. "Here, you better wipe your face off so I can see you better." Josh hoped the man would introduce himself so he wouldn't look foolish if it wasn't Geesler.

He had not seen the doctor, who was a longtime friend of the family, for five years. Geesler was an archeologist and pilot who had learned to fly during World War II.

The man reached out his shaky hand, took the cloth, and wiped his face and gray hair.

Meanwhile Josh began picking up the scattered papers. Under a pile of those papers he found a pair of broken eyeglasses. The frames were bent and one of the lenses was missing. The remaining lens was dirty and cracked, like someone had stepped on it. He couldn't find the other lens anywhere, and if he could, it might not be of any use.

Josh walked over to the old man who was still sitting on the ground. "Here's what's left of your glasses."

"Thank you, young man. I'm Dr. Easton Geesler by the way." Dr. Geesler's fingers felt the frames. "Oh ... my glasses seem to be missing a ... You can't find it over there, can you?"

"Dr. Geesler? I'm sorry I didn't recognize you with all that blood on your face. I'm Josh ... Joshua Powers."

Easton Geesler slipped the remains of his glasses onto his nose. He closed the eye on the side with the missing lens and squinted around the cracks in the broken one; carefully studying the face bending over him.

"Joshua Powers? Joshua Powers! How are you, lad? As you can see I have met with a minor misfortune. Help me to my feet."

"I think you better stay down."

"Nonsense, Joshua, help me up." The old man staggered and almost fell as Josh grabbed his arm to steady him. "Well, maybe I should take it easy for a while."

They walked together to the wooden bench where Geesler wiped more blood off his face with the already blood-soaked handkerchief Josh had given him. Josh checked Geesler's head to make sure the bleeding had stopped.

"What happened, Mr. Geesler?"

"I really don't know who could have done this to me. Ah ... Ah ... Yes. Yes, that's it. I do know who did this terrible deed." Geesler got up on his wobbly feet. "It was those awful scoundrels who attacked me." He flipped through the papers Josh had picked up. "Uh-hum ... Uh-hum ... Uh-hum."

Geesler continued with his "uh-hum" the whole time and seemed unaware Josh was there. Those dirty papers seemed important to him. Finally, Geesler stopped. "It's gone. It's gone." The hand holding the papers dropped down to his side. He looked up and stared across the dry lakebed.

"What's gone, Mr. Geesler?" Josh waited for an answer but Geesler's face was a blank.

This disturbed Josh.

"We must go over there." Geesler still stared across the lake.

"Over where, Mr. Geesler?"

The old man came to life. He straightened his papers like he was sitting at a desk and walked to his suitcase lying open in the dirt. He folded his clothes, put them inside, and laid the papers on top. Carefully he closed the suitcase, latched it shut, then headed toward the airplane.

"Joshua, we must go over there." Geesler pointed across the lake at a black speck as he climbed into the back seat of the airplane. He buckled his seatbelt, and looked straight ahead.

Josh shook his head. First the old man seemed comatose, then everything was fine. Still puzzled, he crawled into the plane, started the engine, and taxied back up the runway.

"You don't need to taxi all the way out. Put the power in and we'll check the magnetos while we're doing our takeoff roll," Geesler said.

Josh pushed the throttle forward and steered the plane down the runway. The engine ran fast enough to check both mags as the airplane left the ground. He pulled back on the stick and started to climb, but he felt Geesler on the backseat controls.

"Too high, Joshua," Geesler yelled over the engine. "We must sneak up on them. Please take the controls and fly low." Geesler pushed forward on the stick so the plane went down.

But Josh pulled back to keep the plane from hitting the ground. He guessed they were fifty feet above the lakebed. Though the airspeed indicator showed they were only flying at ninety miles per hour, the plane's speed seemed faster.

"Where are we going, Mr. Geesler?"

"We're going after the people who stole my map."

"What map?"

"The map I made to tell me where I can find the Sword of David used to take Goliath's head off."

"What would David's sword be doing in the middle of Nevada?" Josh was beginning to have doubts about Geesler.

By the time they flew halfway across the lakebed, Josh worried about what could happen next.

"There ... there they are, off to the right. Near the truck!" Geesler shouted.

"What do you want me to do?" Just when the last word came out of Josh's mouth, Geesler grabbed the controls and veered the airplane to the right. They were headed for the black pickup on the white dry lake.

"Do they have guns?" Josh asked.

"Guns? Guns. Yes, I think they do have guns, but they won't use them." Geesler tried to focus on the truck with one eye closed and the other squinting through the broken lens.

"So they do have guns?" It was the last thing Josh wanted to hear.

The young pilot pulled back on the stick, struggling with Geesler for control of the plane, keeping them at a safe altitude. He could see the old black pickup truck, but where were the people and how did they get stuck in the middle of the lakebed? Then he saw them. Two people dressed in black, pulled their heads out from under the hood—one young woman and the other, an older man.

When the plane roared by, ten feet over-head, both fell to the ground. The man quickly regained composure and shook his fist at the plane, which flew too close, stirring up white dust. The girl appeared to be fifteen or sixteen, not much older than Josh.

Geesler pulled back on the stick and the plane started a steep climb. When it slowed to almost a stall, he stepped on the rudder pedal and turned the plane around, pointing it at the pickup.

Josh grabbed the stick and pulled as hard as he could to keep from crashing. Both the girl and her angry companion took another dive as Geesler rolled the plane to the right, pointing it across the lakebed.

"That will do it. You may take the controls, Joshua. Fly us to the spot right in front of the nose of the plane, if you will please."

"Mr. Geesler, I think I better do the rest of the flying today because of ... of your broken glasses," Josh said. Geesler's flying skills were impressive but Josh actually wasn't sure if the old man could see very well.

"Yes, quite right Joshua. That would be splendid."

"Where are we going?"

"We are going to my cabin to look for the map."

"The map? I thought you said those two people took the map."

"They might have, but I have to be certain."

Josh rolled his eyes as they flew close to the ground, the way he liked it. He couldn't see much, but it made him feel like he was going fast, which required his close attention.

The hill on the edge of the lake came into view. Josh pulled back on the stick and climbed to get a better look. He started a slow turn around the hill, trying to locate Geesler's cabin. It was about a mile by air from the lake, and he could only spot parts of a trail.

As Josh prepared to land, he could see from a distance the black pickup still on the lake and a military helicopter flying on the other side. Josh reached up and changed the channel on his radio.

"Army helio, this is Piper 2-3 Juliet-Papa. Do you read me? Over."

Nothing.

He tried several other channels, but no

response. The helicopter flew back and forth, and finally in the opposite direction.

Josh throttled back. The plane touched ground without a bump—as smooth as going down a kid's slide in a park.

"Nicely done, Joshua. Nicely done." Geesler patted him on the back.

Chapter 2

Josh stretched as he exited the plane. The clean, calm morning air, and familiar smell of white alkali hung over the desert.

"We better get going." Geesler crawled out of the back seat.

"Mr. Geesler, how far is it?"

"It might be two miles up to the cabin. It won't take any time at all to get there."

"Think I better stay here with the airplane. We don't have anything to tie it down and I'm afraid something might happen to it."

"Well ... Yes, why don't you do that." Geesler turned to go up the trail.

This was the first time Josh got a good look at Geesler. He was pale, and tired-looking, and his broken glasses didn't help. Half of his head, and half of his face were sunburned, and his shirt was only partly tucked into his pants. It was not like him at all.

"On second thoughts ... I'll go with you," Josh said.

"Splendid, we will take the harder route then, so we can get there in no time."

Josh took his hat off, and wiped the sweat from his forehead. "I think I better do something first." He reached into the back seat, pulled the stick, grabbed the seatbelt and locked it around the stick. Then he slipped the tail-lockout (which he took from the compartment behind the rear seat) into place at the tail of the plane. He turned to Geesler. "We better push the plane over to the edge of the dry lake."

Somehow they managed to get the Piper off the dry lakebed and into the small brush. Now all they needed was something to block the wheels. Josh collected two small rocks, a piece of wood, a piece of old rusted metal, and a spring off an old car.

After he blocked the wheels Josh closed the doors and remembered to pick up the canteen from the bench.

"Which way do we go, Mr. Geesler?"

"Let's just go straight up the mountain. It's not very far, you know."

It was a steep climb and Josh set out at a good pace. One hundred yards up, however, Geesler slowed down. He could only take five steps, then he had to stop and pant; take another five steps, stop and pant. Finally, he stooped over, breathing heavily.

Josh ran back down to encourage him. "It's really steep, isn't it, Mr. Geesler?"

"Yes ... it is, Joshua." Geesler could only get out one word between breaths. "It's ... very ... steep."

"We'll slow down a bit." Josh sat next to Geesler on the rock.

"You know what I do when I labor up a trail like this? I recite the Psalms." The old man took another deep breath. "Bless the Lord, oh my soul and all that is within me, bless His holy name!

"How old are you, Mr. Geesler?" Josh tried to change the subject.

"Bless the Lord oh my soul and forget not all his benefits." Geesler put up his hand and continued reciting the Psalm. "Who forgives all your iniquities and heals all your diseases. I am eighty-three years old, Joshua. And I have memorized one Psalm for every year I've been alive. I'm glad I won't live to be one-hundred and nineteen." Geesler chuckled. He continued. "Who redeems your life from destruction."

"Destruction? How long have you known my dad by the way?" Josh cleared his throat and looked the other way.

"Who crowns you with loving kindness and tender mercies, who satisfies your mouth with good things, so that your youth is renewed like the eagle's." Geesler put down his hand and smiled. He looked at Josh and whispered, "I believe I have known your folks for about thirty years. I knew them long before you came along. You're fifteen or sixteen aren't you?"

"Just fifteen."

"Fifteen. Well, you're a good pilot for a lad your age."

Josh blushed as he looked down.

"I remember when I was fifteen. We lived in a little town in Scotland—North Berwick. Are you familiar with that town? Lovely place. We did not have much."

Josh truly wanted to hear the story, but he needed to get to the cabin and see if the map was there. But he decided to let the doctor talk, if that's what it took to keep him going. Josh helped him to his feet.

They trekked up the mountain. All the while Josh kept a close eye on Geesler who continued to rest, pant and talk. Josh checked his watch just before they came to the top of the hill where the cabin stood.

"See now. It was not that far after all, was it?" Geesler continued to pant.

The cabin had an outhouse and most of the windows were covered with plywood. The yard was covered with one-hundred-year-old-mining junk.

Geesler took a key out of his pocket and unlocked the big, rusty padlock. "Come in. Come in," he said with glee.

Josh wondered why Geesler bothered to lock such a rundown place. There was no one around for a hundred miles except the two people with the broken-down truck.

Geesler pushed open the door and stood to one side. "After you, Joshua."

Josh ducked, brushing a cobweb off his face, and cautiously stepped into the cabin. It was surprisingly neat even if the floor was dirt. It was swept dirt, but it was still dirt. An army cot with torn, old army blankets, rested against the back wall. Opposite the cot stood a table covered with books, papers, and files.

"Sit down. Sit down, please." Geesler pulled out a wooden chair with a broken wicker seat. "Can I get you anything? Soup?" He took a can of soup from the shelf above the table. "I have a can opener, a bowl, and a spoon."

"No thanks." Josh took his canteen off his neck and sat down. "Would you like a drink, Mr. Geesler?"

"Yes I would, thank you." Geesler held up a cup.

Josh filled it with water and then took a drink from the canteen.

"Ahhhhh ... That does it." Geesler took his cup of water and rummaged through the books, papers, and files.

In the center of the room was an old, black, metal barrel laying on its side. A hole was punched through the side of the barrel for a stovepipe that went up through the open beams of the roof. It appeared to be the only source for heating and cooking.

"Is this going to take a long time?" Josh slid down to the floor, leaned against the wall, and closed his eyes.

"Here it is." Geesler laughed heartily. "They didn't get it after all."

Josh opened one eye and stared at Geesler. "You found the map already?"

"It was right where I left it this morning. I didn't know I left it here, of course, but it was here all along. You know, at my age you tend to forget things." Geesler straightened up a few things in the cabin. "Well, Joshua, that does it. We better get on our way."

Josh headed for the door. "Another drink, Mr. Geesler, before we go?"

"One must be careful how much one drinks when one lives without running water." Geesler had a good chuckle.

"Yes, quite," Josh said with his best British accent.

Geesler locked the door behind them and took a look around. Mining equipment littered the surrounding hills, which were covered with mine shafts, tailings, and junk. Geesler's old cabin was the only building still standing. All the others were nothing but ruins.

"This place looks frightful, doesn't it?" Geesler whispered. "This mining district was built about 1890 and really boomed. Lasted about a year and a half, then went bust. ... Well, we better get going so we can search for the sword and fly home."

They started down the trail as Geesler re-cited yet another Psalm. Josh walked ahead, moving far enough so he couldn't hear Geesler's recital of 83 Psalms. He kept looking for his plane to come into sight.

Twenty more minutes of downhill walking finally brought Josh back to the white, dry lake-bed where, to his surprise, he found the plane. *Who could have moved it? It couldn't have rolled by itself,* he thought. *I blocked the tires.* He turned in every direction but there wasn't a soul in sight. Josh peeked into the plane through the open door.

"My battery! It's gone!" He flung his canteen to the ground. Running back up the hill Josh found Geesler sitting on a rock, singing.

"This country is beautiful, isn't it Joshua?"

"You better come quickly, Mr. Geesler. Somebody moved the plane and stole my battery! They didn't re-block the wheels or anything."

Geesler slowly raised his sunburned head and squinted at Josh through the broken lens of his glasses. "Well, well, well. They did that, did they? It doesn't really matter, we can still start the plane and it will run fine."

"Who did this?" Josh's fists flailed, his voice rose an octave higher.

"Why those two people, the two people we buzzed in your airplane."

Josh calmed himself down and helped Geesler to his feet. Back down the hill they went. When they reached the bottom Josh picked up his canteen.

"Now, when you take hold of the propeller," Geesler instructed, "don't wrap your fingers around it.

Let them lie flat. Then say, 'Switch off.' And I will say it back to you. Do you understand?"

Josh nodded and assisted Geesler into the back seat. He was afraid to start the plane this way without his dad. He had seen his father do it from time to time, but had never done it himself.

"First," Geesler continued, "you pull the propeller through two or three times to clear the engine. You will then say, 'Switch on, throttle on,' and I will repeat that to you. When the switch is on and throttle opened then the engine should start. Any questions?"

Josh shook his head. He wanted to be in the airplane where the pilot belonged, but he knew Geesler was too weak to start the plane this way.

"Switch off!" Josh shouted.

"Switch off, throttle off," came the reply.

Josh reached forward like he was touching a hot stove; his hands barely on the propeller. Very gently, he pulled the engine through. The propeller went a quarter of the way around and stopped.

"That's it, Joshua! Keep it up!"

Josh pulled one more time. The engine went about a quarter of a turn again.

"One more time, Joshua! One more time!"

Josh stepped a little closer and pulled one more time. The propeller turned over and the engine made a complete turn.

Josh wiped the sweat off his forehead. "Okay! Switch on!" He hoped his voice didn't crack as much as he thought it did.

"Switch on! Throttle opened," Geesler shouted.

Josh stared at the propeller like it was a poisonous snake. His hands shook when he placed his hands on the it—careful not to wrap his fingers around it. Then he pulled and jumped back. The propeller turned about a quarter of the way, then kicked backward.

"Switch off!" yelled Geesler. "You must turn the propeller through three times to clear the fuel out of the engine."

"Switch off!"

"Switch off, throttle closed."

Josh took the propeller in both hands. This time pulling it through to make a full circle. He did the same thing two more times.

Josh sighed as he turned his baseball hat sideways. "Switch on, throttle opened." He had a little more authority in his voice.

"Switch on, throttle opened." Geesler repeated.

Josh tried not to think about spinning the propeller this time. He put his hands on the prop and pulled. Nothing happened. He shook his head. "Switch on?"

"Yes, the switch is still on. Go ahead and give it a pull."

Reaching up, Josh grabbed the prop and pulled it through. The engine backfired, smoked, and sputtered to life.

Geesler advanced the throttle. But the spinning propeller seemed to suck Josh in. As he tried to jump away, he slipped and fell. He kicked and screamed, finally managing to crawl to safety, away from the propeller.

Then, unexpectedly, the engine stopped. Josh peeked under the plane. Someone in combat boots stood on the other side of the plane. Josh tiptoed around the front, not wanting to get too close. *Probably the owner of the broken-down pickup,* he thought. Josh did his best to put on his unafraid-friendly voice. "Hi. How you doing?"

"Not good, fool!" The man scratched his black beard. He didn't look at Josh when he spoke. "This old man tried to take our heads off out there. We had to hide for our lives." The piece of car-spring, that had blocked the wheels, was in his hand. It hung down to his side like a weapon. "Get
out of the plane, Geesler."

"You know Dr. Geesler?" Josh stepped toward Geesler to help him.

"Stay right there!" The man, dressed in black jeans and shirt, pointed the car-spring at Josh. And the handle of an automatic handgun stuck out of his waist band.

While the man's focus was on Josh, Geesler reached forward to take the key out of the plane. Josh wisely kept the man's attention. "Where's the girl?" he asked.

"Yes, where's my daughter?" Geesler yelled.

"Where you can't find her."

Daughter? Josh raised his eyebrows. "Are you the one that took the battery out of my plane?"

"Yeah, what are you going to do about it, boy?"

Josh could feel the heat rising in his body. *Don't call me boy.* It was silly, but it angered him. He wanted to jump the guy, but he was much smaller and definitely outgunned. Still, he had successfully diverted the man's attention long enough for Geesler to get the key and drop it under the seat.

Geesler crawled out of the back, put his hand on the man's shoulder and let himself down.

Josh was puzzled. The two seemed awfully familiar with each other.

"Roy, where's Brenda?" asked Geesler. "Oh, by the way Joshua, this is my colleague, Roy Abdullah Al-Razi. I brought him to this country from Iraq after I found the sword."

"I was looking for the map. Where is it?" Roy Al-Razi's fists opened and closed more than once.

Josh knew they were in trouble.

Chapter 3

"Well, I have the map right here." Geesler said. "But I'm not going to tell you where the sword is. You'll have to find that yourself."

Al-Razi grabbed the map. Then he turned and walked away. "You stay right here." He aimed the carspring at Josh. Satisfied that Geesler and Josh wouldn't try to escape, Al-Razi disappeared behind a huge boulder.

"Mr. Geesler, why did you give him the map? Why didn't you tell him you didn't have it?" Josh's face turned red.

"Why Joshua, that would be telling a lie. I don't tell lies. When he asked, I decided to give it to him."

"Why didn't you leave it in the cabin? We could have been halfway home by now?"

"I didn't want him breaking down my door, and going through all my things."

I guess that broken-down cabin must be important to him, Josh thought. *It's probably all he owns. Maybe the sword is hidden there as well.* "Is the sword—"

"Edna! There you are!" Geesler interrupted Josh.

"The name is Brenda!" The girl, short and slightly overweight, snapped at the old man as she eyed Josh from head to foot. She straightened out her black miniskirt and winked at Josh.

"Oh yes, I am very sorry, my dear." Geesler cleared his throat. "Brenda, you remember Joshua Powers don't you?"

"Yeah, I remember him from El Salvador."

Just then Al-Razi reappeared from behind the boulder. His black hair was unkempt; his black beard, unruly. And the black clothes on his thin frame made his skin seem paler than snow. "We've decided to take you back to the cabin and look for the sword." He tied a black bandanna around his head.

Josh remained silent.

"You're kinda cute." Brenda stood nearby still looking at Josh.

"He's a baby!" Al-Razi, who looked to be about thirty-five years old, grabbed her arm.

"Shut up, Roy. I'm only a couple of years older than him."

Al-Razi and Brenda both wore the same T-shirt with bright yellow letters spelling out the band name, "Mockers," with a short list of towns where the band had played. Her black leggings, and black combat boots with bright pink shoe laces, did nothing for her figure.

Josh turned and walked to the other side of the plane.

"Hey! Where do you think you're going?" Al-Razi raised his weapon.

"I'm just looking for shade."

"I told you, you're coming with us back to the cabin to get the sword. So get moving."

Josh headed for the open door of the plane and pulled out the canteen from behind the rear seat. He started to put the strap around his neck, when Al-Razi snatched the canteen from him.

"Thanks, man." Al-Razi smirked. "I'll need this water for the trip."

Josh was actually thankful someone else was going to carry it. He reached down, shut the door of the airplane, walked to the trailhead, and waited.

"Let's get going then." Geesler's voice was pleasant and steady.

Josh let Brenda go ahead of him. Geesler followed Josh. Al-Razi walked behind them all, swinging the car spring through the brush.

Unbeknownst to Al-Razi, Geesler decided to follow the long trail around the mountain, giving Josh enough time to plan his escape. Though Josh considered that Al-Razi had a gun, he looked for places to slip off and disappear. But the desert had sagebrush, which wouldn't hide a small dog.

An hour later, Al-Razi took the last gulp from the canteen and tossed it aside. Josh picked it up.

"What do you want an empty canteen for, boy?" Al-Razi chuckled.

"We're going to need water soon. The can-teen will come in handy, don't you think?"

"Whatever."

"Yeah, whatever." Josh continued on the trail, trying not to get furious.

"You don't like Roy very much, do ya?" Brenda whispered.

"Um, you mean the guy who kidnapped us? No, not very much. And I don't like the way he talks to us."

"Yeah, he's a real jerk."

"What are you doing out here with him?"

Brenda had no reply. She looked away and pointed out across the lakebed. "Is ... Isn't it beautiful?"

Before Josh could respond, she continued.

"My mom ... my mom and I didn't get along really well. We always fought. And my dad lives in this desert by himself. Do you have trouble with your parents?"

"Not those kind of problems. Actually, I get along with both my parents."

"You're very lucky, Josh. I wish I got—"

"Hey!" Al-Razi interrupted. "What are you two children talking about? Your wedding plans?"

"We're talking about our home life. Not that you care. And stop calling us names." Josh hung his head.

Al-Razi stepped forward, beat on his chest,-and reached for his gun.

Josh took a step back. His heart thumped with fear, but mostly anger.

Al-Razi, grabbed Josh's shirt from behind and yanked him violently. "Don't speak to me like that again, infidel. I will call you what I want. I can kill you like I would kill a rat." He let go of Josh's shirt but kept up the tirade. "I have come to this country for one mission and I will kill anyone who gets in my way."

Brenda stood still, her shaking hand over her tightlipped mouth

More than likely, Josh thought, *Al-Razi was the one who hit Geesler on the head. And if Al-Razi was capable of that he would probably have no problem hitting a fifteen-year-old kid who annoyed him.* Josh decided to do what he was told.

Al-Razi grabbed Brenda's arm and forced her to walk behind him, then got in line behind Josh who picked up the pace, creating a large distance between them. He checked his watch. It had been two hours since they left the airplane. The cabin had to be close as they walked through the rubble of an abandoned town with boarded-up mineshafts, broken-down cabins, and abandoned buildings. This was a ghost town. Finally, the one standing cabin—Geesler's cabin—came in to view. This time it looked good to Josh. "There's the cabin," he said.

Geesler panted heavily. "Yes. Home."

"Hurry up and open the door, Geesler, or I'll tear it down." Al-Razi yelled out his demands.

"Yes, yes ... I will." Geesler fumbled around with the large ring of keys and unlocked the door.

Al-Razi crowded in front of him and pushed the door open. "Where's the water? I'm thirsty!"

"I don't have any. Well, not much anyway." Geesler took down a small bottle of water from a shelf, and held it out. "There's only enough water for one."

Al-Razi grabbed the bottle. He guzzled most of it before giving Brenda the last few drops.

Brenda peeked over the top of the dark, brown bottle at Josh, then threw it into the corner across the room. "That took care of my thirst." She shrugged her shoulders, raised her eyebrows, and grinned.

"Edna, why? Why are you doing this?" Geesler asked with a sigh.

"It's Brenda now, old man. Can't you get that through your thick head? Brenda!"

Al-Razi suddenly shoved Geesler's papers and books off the table. He laughed hideously.

"Roy! Why do you have to do that? Leave my things alone!"

"Roy, leave my things alone." Al-Razi mimicked. One hand was on his hip as he threw his head back and saluted like a victorious general after a glorious battle. "Let's start looking for the sword." He headed out the door. "I suppose you're not going to help us?"

"Your assumption is correct," Geesler replied.

Al-Razi walked out the door with Brenda. Geesler followed close behind. But he turned to look at

36

one of the mineshafts, then twisted the other way to look at another one, and walked back toward the cabin.

Folding the map, Al-Razi shrugged, made his way to the tunnel and began pulling the wood nailed across the entrance.

Geesler's squinted through the cracks of his glasses to see what Al-Razi was up to. The old man reached into his back pocket, pulled out the dirty, blood-stained handkerchief, and wiped his sun-burnt head.

Al-Razi pulled down enough wood to make a hole to crawl through. "Do you have a flashlight, old man?"

"No, I don't."

With a loud grunt, Al-Razi stomped back to the cabin. Several crashes and clangs later he came back with a flashlight. Pointing the light at Geesler, he mumbled something in Arabic as he passed by on his way to the mine. He crawled through the opening.

"Brenda, get in here!

"No!"

Al-Razi reappeared and ran toward her. He shone the light in her face then raised the flash-light like he would strike her. "I said, get in there! You better obey me!"

"I don't want to go in the tunnel, it's ... it's dark in there and it could cave in."

Al-Razi glared at her, still holding the flash-light over her head.

"Why don't you leave her out here with me?" Josh said. "She could watch me. After all, I might try to escape if you both go in there."

"Yeah, you'd like that, wouldn't you?" Al-Razi paced for a couple of minutes before he pointed the flashlight at Brenda again. "You stay out here and watch him. If he tries to escape or anything, start screaming.

Al-Razi faced Josh. "You try to escape, I'll find you!" He spun, pointing the metal flashlight at Geesler. "You ... old man! Come with me."

Chapter 4

"Where did you meet this guy?" Josh asked.

Brenda twirled stray strands of hair between her fingers. "I enrolled at a Junior College. He was teaching a class on Muslims in America. I took the class. The rest is history."

"He's a lot older than you, isn't he? Aren't you sixteen or seventeen?"

"He's thirty-two. Isn't he dreamy?"

Josh rolled his eyes. "I don't think I'd call him that." He looked down the hill and back at the entrance of the tunnel. "We should run down the hill to the airplane and get help."

"I wouldn't if I were you." Brenda said.

"Why not? We can be down there in ten minutes and out of here in another five."

"In case you've forgotten, you don't have a battery."

"The battery. Oh yeah. Where is it?"

Brenda smirked. "Wouldn't you like to know? All I have to do is scream and Roy will come running out of the mineshaft."

Josh slumped to the ground; he sat with his back facing Brenda. He never figured she was that attached to Roy. She had said he was a jerk, but she remained loyal. He wondered if Roy had feelings for her or if he was using her.

As Josh sat thinking, Geesler stumbled out of the mineshaft and fell to the ground.

Roy crawled out after him. "Where is the sword, old man? Don't make me look in all these mines." He got up and staggered to where Geesler lay. "Just tell me where it is and you might live to see the sunrise."

"I'm not going to tell you." Geesler covered his mouth and coughed.

Brenda ran to Al-Razi. "Josh wanted me to escape with him while you were in the tunnel, but I stopped him. I told him he didn't have a battery."

Al-Razi's face turned red. He spun and glared at Josh. Marching up to him, Al-Razi raised the flashlight as if to hit him. Josh shielded his head.

"I would beat you if I didn't need you to fly me out of this forsaken place." Al-Razi clenched his teeth.

Josh trembled. His hands became clammy; sweat dripped off his forehead. Crashing a plane in El Salvador was a frightening experience, but this seemed different—out of his control.

Al-Razi pulled a set of handcuffs out of his back pocket. He slipped one end around Geesler's wrist and locked it. "Your daughter was right. You're a stubborn, crazy old man."

Al-Razi then grabbed Josh's arm, pulled him to his feet, and shoved him toward a large metal flywheel. "Sit down and don't move."

"Get up, old man, and come sit here by the boy."

Geesler pushed himself up, hobbled to the rusty wheel and collapsed next to Josh.

Al-Razi took the open end of the handcuff, threaded it around one of the spokes on the fly-wheel, and locked it onto Josh's wrist. "*Now* let's see you escape." He laughed and thumped Josh on the back of the head.

Al-Razi stepped away from them, pulled out Geesler's map and poured his attention over every mineshaft location.

"Woman! Come here. Now!"

Brenda got up slowly. "Don't yell at me like that." Her eyes teared up and her lips quivered.

Al-Razi reached out and pulled her close to him. "I want you to do what I tell you, when I tell you. You're going into that mineshaft with me."

"No! Please don't make me go. I don't want to go in there."

But Al-Razi pushed her toward the tunnel. She struggled to free herself as he wrapped his arm around her waist.

"Somebody stop him, please! I don't want to go!"

"Let her go, you scoundrel!" Geesler yelled.

"And what are you going to do if I don't?"

Josh shook his head. "God, what can I do to stop this guy?" He turned to face Al-Razi who was still dragging Brenda toward the shaft. "Hey Roy! Why don't you take me instead? I'm not afraid to go into the tunnels. You could keep an eye on me and I'll help you look for the sword."

"Stay where you are." Al-Razi reached for his gun.

He forced Brenda to the ground. "Fine. Stay out here with dear daddy then. Don't go anywhere while I'm gone. If they get loose, scream."

Brenda lay on the ground, sobbing and whimpering.

"You disgust me." Al-Razi left her with Josh and her father and strutted toward the tunnel.

Geesler shook his head. "Oh, what a mess I've gotten us into."

"How is this your fault?" Josh asked.

"I should never have enticed them to come out here to look for the Sword of David."

"How did you get the sword out here?"

"Joshua, that is a long story and I don't want to go into it right now."

"Mr. Geesler, do you even have the Sword of King David?"

Geesler leaned over. "I have a confession to make. It is rather embarrassing since it is not like me to lie, but alas, I did. I should not have done it."

Josh waited for Geesler to confess what he lied about. But an uncomfortable silence grew between them as Geesler stared at the mineshaft and minutes passed like hours.

Finally, Geesler let out a sigh and said, "I must tell him the truth."

"What truth?"

"The truth is ... there is no Sword of David. I just wanted to see my daughter and talk her out of any relationship she might have with Roy."

"You mean Al-Razi?

"Yes."

"Why does he want the sword?"

"I don't know. There was something about destroying it on national television to prove God would not—or could not—stop him."

"I guess if you want to tell him the truth we should pray for some courage."

"Maybe we should."

Josh bowed his head and placed his hand on Geesler's arm. "Heavenly Father, give Mr. Geesler the courage to tell Al-Razi the truth and for Brenda to know that her father loves her. Protect us all. In Jesus' name, Amen."

When he opened his eyes, Al-Razi stood over him ... scowling.

"You pray?" Al-Razi snapped. "Your God does not answer. He never answers. You pray for truth?

What truth do you have to tell me? And where is Brenda?"

"She was right over by the cabin a minute ago," Josh said.

"Roy, the truth is that I wanted to see my daughter so I lied about the—" A blood-curdling scream from behind one of the old abandoned buildings interrupted Geesler.

Al-Razi stood frozen, his widened eyes fixed on Geesler.

"It's Brenda," Geesler yelled. "Go find out what is wrong with her, Roy! Quickly!"

Al-Razi hesitated, then raced toward the old building and around the corner. In a few seconds he came back with Brenda who was limping and crying.

"It bit me. It bit me."

"What bit you?" Josh asked.

"A snake! I think it was a rattlesnake."

"Roy, you should find the snake and see what kind it was." Josh nodded.

Al-Razi stared at him. "I don't like vipers."

"I don't either, but we need to find out what kind it was. Let me loose and I'll find it."

Al-Razi fumbled in his pocket for the keys to the handcuffs. Reluctantly, he reached down and unlocked Josh from the wheel.

"Brenda, let me see where you were bit." Josh pulled her hand off her leg, took ahold of her and looked her right in the eye. "I have to look at the bite."

Josh tore her black leggings and found two bite marks a fraction of an inch apart, with some swelling. "It does look like a rattlesnake. Mr. Geesler, do you have a snakebite kit?"

"Yes, I have one. I'll get it." Geesler ran into the cabin with handcuffs dangling from one wrist and returned with the kit.

Josh was familiar with the kit having used one when his family lived in the jungle of Central America. The kit contained an Extractor pump, and four different-sized plastic suction cups. Also included were four alcohol pads and three band-aides.

Brenda screamed and kicked but Josh managed to attach the suction cups.

"We have to do this before we get you to the hospital. Mr. Geesler, we better go find that snake and confirm if it was a rattler."

"I'll go find it, Joshua. You stay here with Brenda." Geesler picked up a stick and looked for the snake.

Al-Razi remained useless, standing like a statue at the corner of the old building.

Five minutes later, Geesler returned. "I couldn't find the snake, but I do think it was a rattler. Look at the swelling. Her leg has swollen more in the last five minutes. Now what do we do?"

"We get her to the hospital in Bishop. It's about an hour from here." I can fly her there."

"I don't think I can carry her," Geesler said.

"Al-Razi, we need your help." Josh was no longer afraid to make any demands.

Al-Razi snapped out of his trance and picked Brenda up. "Move! You two go first!"

Josh jumped out of the way and took the shortcut back to the airplane. It was steeper, but much faster.

When they reached the plane Josh opened the door. "Put her in the back seat." He clicked her seatbelt, slipped the ear-phones on her head, and hopped into the pilot's seat.

"No!" Josh threw his hands in the air. "The battery! Where's the battery?"

Chapter 5

Al-Razi took slow deep breaths; hands on his hips and a frown on his face. "The battery is behind that bush."

"Go get it!" Josh yelled. "Hurry!"

"Get it yourself."

Josh shook this head and ran to the bush. The weight of the battery seemed as heavy as the plane itself. He slid it under the front seat and fastened it into place—put the positive side of the battery cable on first, and tightened it with a wrench, then did the same with the negative side.

Josh was about to jump back into the plane, when Al-Razi put his hand on Josh's chest. "After the girl is delivered, if you want to see the old man alive again, you better come back and get us. Do you understand? Don't talk to anyone. If I find out you did, I will kill both of you. No one will find your bodies out here." Al-Razi now had Geesler by the collar with the pistol pointed at his head.

"I understand. I'll be back."

"You better!" Al-Razi stuck his gun into Geesler's back and pushed him out of the way.

Josh entered the plane. "That guy is just plain bad." He opened the window, stuck his head out, called, "clear prop," and hit the starter button.

The airplane turned over a few times and started. He looked at his gauges, ran the engine up, and checked the magnetos. Convinced every-thing was working, he pushed the throttle forward. Josh glanced over his shoulder. Al-Razi and Geesler still stood in the same position.

The plane rolled across the lakebed. As it reached eighty miles-per-hour, Josh pulled back gently on the stick. They climbed to three hundred feet and leveled off. Josh turned the plane toward the pass taking them to Bishop.

Brenda moaned. "I feel like I'm going to puke."

"There's a sick sack in the pouch on the back of my seat. Reach down and get it." Josh adjusted his headset and turned off the intercom. He did *not* want to hear her throw up. A few minutes after she had pulled out the sick sack Josh turned the intercom back on. "How do you feel now?"

"I'm not as nauseated as I was, but my leg is swelling even more. It's turning black and ugly."

"Bishop is about forty-five minutes away. They have a hospital. Try to stay awake." Josh looked for the narrow and high pass to get through the mountains.

The White Mountains were too high for him to fly over. And though he had flown through the pass before, it was hard to see from this side.

"Brenda, how are you doing back there?" Josh searched for the highway, but saw nothing.

"I'm okay, my leg hurts, but I'm okay."

"By the way, what are you doing running around with Roy? Isn't he too old for you?"

"Yeah, I know. I wanted to get my dad's attention. I wanted to feel like I was loved by a man, and Roy loves me."

"Are you sure? I really don't think he does. I think he's using you."

"Sometimes I think you're right, but—"

"Did he try to comfort you when you got that snake bite, or say take care, goodbye, I'll see you soon? The only thing he did was point a gun at your father's head and shout orders."

"Well, my dad's impossible!" Brenda paused before she spoke again. "But you're right Josh, he didn't say anything to comfort me."

"Brenda, can I tell you something? Josh could feel his heartbeat. "You've probably heard it before."

"What? I shouldn't be going out with a jerk? Yeah, I've heard it before."

"No, that's not it. Brenda ... God loves you and He's got something much better for you." There, he said it. And he was glad she was sitting behind him so he couldn't see her face or she, his—because his was turning red. He continued before Brenda could interrupt.

"God really does love you."

"Yeah I've heard that before too. Why would God love me? Do you believe all that stuff about God sending His Son so we could have eternal life?"

"Yeah, I do. I got lazy about my relationship with God. But God can be trusted. I should know. He helped me rescue my dad from drug lords."

"I don't know, Josh. I don't think God hears me anymore. I've done some bad things."

"So have I, we all have. I don't think anyone is good. That's why we need God."

The conversation changed all of a sudden when Josh spotted the highway running through the pass. "There's the highway!"

Brenda was silent as Josh watched the cars below. She stared out the window, apparently deep in thought.

He flew the plane toward the road. But as he neared the pass he noticed he was too low. He spun the airplane into a steep climb back over the highway, spinning for a couple of dizzy revolutions to gain altitude. When they reached six thousand feet he turned back toward the pass.

"Josh? I think I want God to love me again!"

"What?" Josh flew the plane through the pass before he could switch his brain back to their conversation. "God has always loved you, Brenda."

"I know." Brenda fought back the nausea. "But I want the kind of relationship with God like you have." She covered her mouth and looked at the ugliness of her open wound. "I guess my life's like an open wound. Maybe it's time to come home." A tear rolled down her cheek as she bowed her head. "Dear God, we haven't talked for a long time. Please forgive me. Help my parents to forgive me too. And help me to be the person You want me to be. Please show me how. Amen."

"Amen." Josh cleared his throat. He pushed the talk-button on his microphone when they flew out of the pass. "Bishop Unicom. This is Piper 2-3 Juliet-Papa. Over. Bishop Unicom. This is Piper 2-3 Juliet-Papa. Do you read me? Over."

No answer. Maybe he was too far away or maybe they had stepped out of the office. He would wait to try again later. They were still thirty-five miles from the airport when Josh switched to the emergency channel and tried one more time

"Bishop, this is Piper 2-3 Juliet-Papa. Do you read? Over."

"Piper 2-3 Juliet-Papa, this is Caravan 4-8 Bravo. What is your emergency? Over."

"4-8 Bravo, I have a girl onboard who was bitten by a rattlesnake. We need the paramedics waiting for us at Bishop Airport. Over."

"Copy that, 2-3 Juliet-Papa. I will relay your message to Bishop. How far out are you? Over."

"4-8 Bravo. I'm about twenty minutes from touchdown. Thanks for the relay. Over."

"Roger that."

Josh turned to Brenda. "Are you all right?"

She was slumped back in the seat. Her eyes were closed and she wasn't moving.

"Hang in there. We'll be in Bishop soon."

Still no response.

He only had two thousand feet to ground, which was not enough to dive the plane to get to the airport. Josh gave the airplane more gas to gain speed. As he reached to his left, pushing the throttle forward, the airspeed indicator increased in speed—one hundred and thirty miles per hour. That's as fast as it could fly. He switched his radio back to 122.9, the Unicom frequency.

"Bishop Unicom. This is Piper 2-3 Juliet-Papa, Over."

"Piper 2-3 Juliet-Papa. Hear you have an emergency? Over."

"Bishop, I have a girl with a snakebite. She'll need a ride to the hospital. Can anyone help?"

"Piper 2-3 Juliet-Papa. The paramedics are waiting. What is your ETA?"

"Bishop, we have about five more minutes. It seems she has passed out. She isn't talking anymore. Over."

"Roger. I'll tell the paramedics."

Josh searched frantically for the airport and the paramedic truck. The airport, which served as a fighter-training base in WWII, on the Northeast part of town, should be easy to find. It was a big airport with cross-runways.

He found the windsock on top of the old plywood tower telling him he could land on the cross-runway headed for the tower. The wind blew directly at them, slowing the plane.

"This is Bishop Unicom. We have a piper cub on final approach. It has an emergency. All aircrafts hold your position."

Josh began his final descent. He pulled back on the throttle and slowed the plane to eighty miles-per-hour. The wind blew too hard. "We're not going to make it!" He looked for the red lights of the paramedic truck. *Keep your mind on the landing, Josh ... and the wind.*

When the plane crossed the end of the runway, he was way too high. Josh put the plane into a slip, ridding himself of some altitude. Right before he touched down, he spotted the flashing red lights of the paramedic truck.

Nearing the truck, he pushed the throttle forward, then backed off to a gradual stop. He cut the engine and stepped out.

"Are you old enough to fly this thing?" One of the paramedics asked as he rolled the stretcher next to the plane.

"No, he's not!" A voice bellowed from the back of the crowd.

Josh froze. He knew he wasn't allowed to carry passengers. But this was an emergency, and he didn't think anyone in Bishop would care.

"I'm Mike Williams from the FAA (Federal Aviation Administration). What is your name?"

"I'm Joshua Powers."

"Do you have a pilot's license?"

"Yes sir." Josh fumbled for his black leather wallet. "It's a student pilot's license." He handed his license to the FAA agent, then returned to the paramedics.

"You're not ..." Mike Williams stopped when he realized Josh had walked away.

"How long has she been unconscious?" One of the paramedics checked Brenda's vitals.

"About half an hour," Josh replied.

"Her leg is badly swollen and turning dark brown. We'll get her to the hospital. Do you want to go?" The paramedic loaded Brenda into the ambulance.

"No, I need to fly back and pick up her dad. He's worried about her."

The paramedic nodded as Mike Williams tapped Josh on the shoulder. Josh turned.

"You know of course, you're never supposed to fly passengers, don't you?"

Josh hung his head.

"You also know I can take your license and you won't be able to fly anymore."

Josh nodded.

"Why fly with a passenger?"

"I know it was wrong and I know you can take my license, but it was an emergency. Brenda was bit by a rattlesnake." Josh took a big gulp as Williams stared him down.

"Why didn't her dad fly her in?"

"He broke his glasses and can't see without them. I didn't think he should fly." Josh pleaded his case. "I'm sorry, Mr. Williams, I'll try not to do it again."

"You'll try not to do it again? That's not much comfort." William slapped one hand with Josh's license. "But then again ... I would've done the same thing." Williams handed back the license and smirked. "You probably saved that girl's life. I like to see our pilots saving lives, even when they risk losing their license." He put his hand on Josh's shoulder and whispered, "you know I had to be tough on you, right? Don't want to lose my cushy FAA job."

"Thank you, sir." Josh smiled.

"Fine job, Joshua Powers. Keep up the good work." Mike Williams walked toward his car, got in, and took off.

Josh was glad to see him go as he made his way around the edge of a hangar. Soon he came across an old pilot working on his plane.

"That FAA bird yank your license?" The old pilot cleaned off his greasy tools on his pullover. "All those guys want to do is give you a ration of grief."

"Oh, he's all right," Josh said. "Where can I get some gas? I've got to get going."

"The man to ask is that grey-headed old coot in Building B. He's the FBO and airport manager. He'll help you."

Josh walked to Building B and was about to say hello when the grey-headed old coot beat him to it.

"Hey kid, you did a great job bringing that girl in and radioing in ahead. Nice job."

"Are you Mr. Austin?"

"Sure am. And who might you be?"

"I'm Joshua Powers."

"Joshua Powers? You're Doug Powers' son? How is your dad?" Jerry Austin folded his arms. "Is he still alive? Those savages in Central America didn't boil him or nothing, did they?"

"My dad is fine." Josh chuckled.

"Doug Powers saved my bacon down there in the jungle. Had a plane crash and he rescued me. I owe him big time. Wouldn't let me pay him. And he introduced me to Jesus. Best thing I ever did. Yeah, giving my life to Jesus." Jerry Austin approached Joshua. "So, what can I do for you, young Powers?"

"I need to fly back out to Emerson Lake and pick up a friend. My plane could use some gas. Can you fill it up and let me pay you later?"

"No, but I can fill it up for nothing. Can you handle that?"

"I can handle that."

56

"Remember, I owe your dad big time."

Chapter 6

When Josh left Bishop Airport, with a full tank of gas, he flew through the pass and lowered to three hundred feet above ground. He didn't want to go back to Emerson Dry Lake, but knew he had no choice.

Geesler was still out there with crazy Roy. And rescuing Geesler was Josh's goal. Al-Razi had a gun and wasn't afraid to use it. So he had to be smart. Josh shook his head. *I think I've been shot at enough for a lifetime.*

Near the lakebed, Josh descended to one hundred feet. Maybe he could sneak up on Geesler and Roy. Not much chance of that, but he would try it anyway.

The closer he got to the airport the more his stomach twisted in knots. His eyes located the red flags at the end of the runway. Pulling the throttle back, he slowed the plane and decided to stop right there. He figured he could walk to the bench from the end of the runway.

"Father, no need to tell you that Al-Razi is dangerous. Give Mr. Geesler and me the courage and the chance to escape. Amen."

Josh crept out of the plane. He pulled his cap down over his forehead and walked, stooped over, across the hot lakebed. "Well, here goes."

But one hundred feet from the plane, he straightened up. "This is pointless. A blind man could see me out here."

Al-Razi, however, was nowhere in sight. Josh snuck up to the bench and looked around. He took off his baseball cap and wiped the sweat off his forehead. He thought of all the places Geesler and Al-Razi could be—in one of the mine shafts perhaps; or in Geesler's cabin.

He decided to take a chance and call out. "Mr. Geesler, I'm back! Mr. Geesler, are you there!" No answer. "Oh, man. I do *not* feel like hiking back up to the cabin."

He jogged up the trail anyway, passing a shack where the miners stored explosives.

"What took you so long?" Al-Razi walked out of the shack.

Josh spun around. "Where's Mr. Geesler? We have to get going if we want to get back to Bishop before dark."

"What took you so long?" Roy asked again.

"It takes about an hour to get to Bishop and an hour back. Where's Mr. Geesler?"

"The old man won't be going with you. I will."

The knot in Josh's stomach got tighter. Al-Razi had warned him that he would kill Geesler if he didn't return. Had he kept his word?

"Did you talk to anyone?" Al-Razi, pulled his gun from his waistband.

"No. I didn't talk to anyone or tell anyone. Where is Mr. Geesler?"

"Geesler is ... um ... busy. He can't go. I'm going with you."

Josh crunched his eyebrows together. He stepped through the door of the shack and found Geesler asleep, handcuffed to a bedpost. The room was dark and smelled of diesel fuel.

"Mr. Geesler, are you okay?" Josh knelt by the old man's side.

Geesler opened his eyes slowly. "Joshua, you are back. Is Brenda all right?"

"I really don't know. The paramedics were at the airport and took her to the hospital. Are you okay?"

"I'm fine. Roy tells me he's going with you this time. Something about a mission. I think he's going to blow up a terminal in Los Angeles."

Josh's eyes widened. "What?" He jumped to his feet, spun around, and stomped up to Al-Razi. "Geesler has to get to his daughter! She's in really bad shape!" Josh's voice was shaky as he got close to Al-Razi's face. "And I'm not helping you blow anything up!"

Josh backed away as Al-Razi aimed his gun at him. "Don't you ever, ever speak to me like that again!

Now, you and I are getting into that plane and you *will* fly me out of here! Got it?"

After Al-Razi calmed down, he took the cuffs off Geesler. "That lie about the sword of David has cost me time. Don't leave this shack until you hear the plane go over. Do you hear me?

Geesler nodded. "Joshua, please tell Brenda I love her."

Al-Razi grabbed Josh's arm, and stuck the barrel of the gun against his back. "Let's get out of here!"

"Okay, fine," Josh whispered.

Al Razi shoved Josh all the way back to the plane. "Don't think about doing anything stupid. I'm going to get in the back seat, but I will have my eyes on you. Understand?"

Josh nodded, and grabbed the strut. "Put your seat belt on and leave it buckled the whole flight. We may hit some turbulence in the pass. Keep your feet and hands off the controls, and put that green headset on. That's the intercom."

Josh buckled his seatbelt and bowed his head and prayed like he did on every flight. But this time he felt the gun thrust up into his ribs.

Al-Razi sneered. "Are you praying to your God?"

"Yes, I am."

"Why do you pray to Him?"

"God has saved me many times. Do you ever pray?"

"Yes, of course. We pray during our daily prayer times."

Josh hadn't seen him pray at all. He let it go and went through his preflight checklist—read the chart, reached up to set his altimeter, then ran the controls making sure they all worked.

"Let us go!" Al-Razi was restless. "You are stalling."

Josh turned on the master switch and stuck his head out the window. "Clear prop."

"Who are you talking to, that old man is a half mile away?" Al-Razi laughed.

Josh ignored Al-Razi and pushed the starter button, which brought the plane to life. He took his time, not wanting to leave Geesler behind.

The windsock confirmed he could take off toward the cabin. Josh checked his magnetos then pushed the throttle forward. The airplane began its move down the runway. When it lifted off the ground, Josh held it low until he passed over the shack.

Suddenly, he pulled sharply back on the stick which caused the plane to shoot up into the sky. Then just when it reached the point where it was about to stall, he pushed the stick forward and leveled off.

"What are you doing? What are you doing? You are going to kill us!"

Josh smiled. "We'll reach Bishop in about an hour."

"We are not going to Bishop. I am going to complete my mission."

Josh was sure Al-Razi was going to kill him. But he set a course for Bishop anyway. *This could be my last flight,* he thought, *so might as well try to share God's love with him.*

Josh whispered a prayer. "Father, You said that Your word does not return to You void. Give me the courage and strength to share with this man. Give me the words, Your words, to make a difference. In Jesus' name, Amen."

"Talking to God again?" Al-Razi punctuated his demand with the familiar jab to the ribs.

"I was just praying."

"I used to pray to the same God you are praying to."

"You did?"

"My father was a Christian pastor in Iraq. When the other Muslims drove him out of the country, I could not believe God would let that happen."

"You were a Christian?"

"I *was* a Christian. Now I must prove to the Muslim people I am good enough. That's why I have decided to do this mission."

"Roy." Josh hesitated and paused before he spoke again. "You *are* good enough. God loves you just the way you are. He wants only the best for you. God even knows your name."

"I do not believe God loves me. How could He? He never answered my prayers?"

"My dad says God answers all prayer in His time, not ours."

"Yeah, whatever. My father is still a pastor and tries to get me to believe." Al-Razi pulled at his beard.

"There's a verse in the Bible that says, 'God demonstrates His love toward us while we were yet sinners, Christ died for us.'"

The intercom went dead.

Josh was surprised he even remembered that verse. He continued to pray softly. "Father, I don't know what else to say. Help me say the right thing. Help me know when to talk and when to be quiet. Lord, keep me calm and peaceful. Maybe I planted a seed. Amen."

Josh flew on in silence.

But the trip through the pass had Al-Razi frazzled. Turbulence thrashed the airplane up and down, and back and forth. It was like being inside a washing machine.

Coming out of the pass proved no better when they ran into a strong headwind. The turbulence didn't stop. It got worse. Al-Razi held on with both hands, the gun bouncing on his lap. When they flew over Bishop, Josh stayed near the mountains avoiding the airport and kept flying south. "So where do we go from here?" Josh asked.

"Los Angeles International Airport."

"We can't land this plane at an international airport."

"We must. Why do you say we cannot?"

"It's a restricted airport. This plane flies too slow. Big jets fly in there."

"We will declare an emergency."

"We can't do that. They will turn us away." Josh was lying. It wasn't something he did often.

Al-Razi sat in silence, still staring out of the window, gripping the sides of the door. Whenever the airplane dropped, his grip tightened. His expression turned to horror: eyes wide; skin color pukey pale.

The next airport was at Big Pine, but Josh had one more trick up his sleeve. "There's a little airport up ahead. Do you want to land and wait for the wind to die down?"

"No! Not there. You told someone to meet us there, didn't you? No, we will not stop."

"Okay, but the wind is getting worse as the sun goes down." Josh shook his head. "I'm not supposed to fly at night, either."

The plane bounced and turned as they flew down the valley. Dust whirled into the sky like it was the end of the world, making it hard for Josh to locate the ground. He let the airplane descend closer to the ground so he could see. It didn't help. The dust and wind grew violent. They flew on, bouncing and dropping, wings dancing in the wind. It was a dog fight to keep the plane in the air.

Moans and shrieks came over the intercom. "There! Land there!" Al-Razi could barely get the words out.

"There's no airport there," Josh shouted.

"Yes! Look! Look down there!"

Josh squinted through the dust. There *was* an airport—an abandoned airport with a paved runway marked by four giant X's.

"It's the airport for the Manzanar Japanese Internment Camp." Josh wanted to get on the ground quickly. "The runway has been there since World War II. It's probably rutted and broken."

"You must land!" Al-Razi panicked.

Josh made a wide turn to the left picking up speed when they got to the downwind leg. He circled the runway until the plane lined up. Pulling back on the throttle, the plane sputtered. Josh pushed the throttle back in and began a power descent. Close to the old asphalt runway, he pulled back hard on the throttle one more time. The wind howling down the runway meant he didn't have to fight a crosswind. Finally, the airplane touched down and stopped rolling in seventy-five feet.

"Let me out of here!" Al-Razi pounded on the door.

Josh reached for the handle and opened it. The bottom half fell down against the side of the plane as Josh held up the top half. Al-Razi couldn't squeeze through fast enough.

The forty-mile-per-hour gales forced Al-Razi's body to twist and turn as he walked away, fighting the wind with every step.

Josh saw it as his chance to escape. He left the door open, and put the power in. The plane rolled. He hunched over in his seat expecting bullets to rip through the plane. One hundred feet down the runway, with help from the wind, the plane leaped into the sky.

He glanced back over his shoulder. There, in the wind and dust, he spotted Al-Razi—arms outstretched and firing his gun. The muzzle flashes spun Josh in his seat. He slouched over. Gunfire continued. But Josh was safely out of reach.

Chapter 7

The forty-mile-per-hour tailwind pushed Josh back toward Bishop. He was free. "Father, thank You for protecting me."

But as he glanced out the window, he gasped. A bullet hole, about the size of his finger, had punctured the gas tank, though no liquid seemed to be seeping out.

He knew the hole could enlarge. He would have to keep an eye on it. A bullet makes a small hole going in and a larger, ragged hole going out. Depending on how large and ragged it was, it could bring the plane down.

Fuel could be collecting in the wing. He wondered what the top of the wing looked like. The fabric covering on the wings was stretched tight, but the hole might be large enough to cause a problem for the air going over the top of the wing. The top of the wing is critical. It's what made the airplane fly.

"God, please help me get on the ground." Josh searched for a safe place to land. He found nothing but piles of lava rocks and tall brush.

He thought about going on to Big Pine, but the Big Pine airport was too far. What if the fabric on the top of the wing ripped off? He had to get the airplane on the ground, fast.

Finally, he spotted a dirt road running north and south, the direction he was flying. His concern now was to keep the plane from blowing away. One more pass over the road allowed him to locate anything he could use to patch the hole on top of the wing.

Pulling back on the throttle Josh let the airplane glide down to one hundred feet. He flew another ten minutes until he came over a rise in the ground. That's when he noticed a small building with a cement slab out in front. The slab covered the whole width of the road.

The building was perfect for him to examine the plane in and hopefully make necessary repairs.

Josh headed into the wind—pushing more power in so the plane would stay in the air. Close to the building, he let the plane settle down to the ground. He taxied up to the building, parking in the back to stay out of the wind.

He killed the engine and held the brakes as the plane rocked back and forth but it didn't roll. Josh jumped out and went to the door in the front of the building. It stood wide open. He stuck his head inside. The dark, dust-filled room was littered with papers and he could see where the scale had been removed.

A large red barrel with "Gasoline" written on its side, stood in the corner of the room. *I can use this to stand on*, he thought. *I've got to get on top of the wing somehow.*" The barrel was empty, which would make it easier for him to haul to the plane.

He found three big rocks to steady the wheels already turned by the wind. Then he examined the underside of the wing where the bullet entered. Josh stuck his finger through the hole and felt the crease in the side of the fuel tank. Though the crease was bigger than he thought, Josh blew out a sigh of relief. "Thank You, Lord, that it didn't hit the tank."

Standing on top of the barrel Josh inspected the hole on the upper part of the wing. "Un-believable!" He scratched his head. "This hole is as big as my fist." *Man. I wonder why the bullet didn't go into the tank?* God had protected him for sure. His dilemma now was to find something to patch the hole with.

"Speed tape!" Josh slapped the side of his head. "That's why Dad said to always carry it in the airplane."

A new roll of speed tape was behind his seat. He wondered how it would work on the wing. It would be tested in a hundred-mile-per-hour wind. *Shouldn't make a difference,* he thought, *since they use it to patch holes on military jets.*

He dusted off the wing with a rag—from the hole on the top, down around to the front of the wing, back past the entrance hole on the bottom. He made sure the tape would stick.

A foot of speed tape he stuck to the bottom of the wing, then rubbed it to make sure it was attached. Climbing on the barrel, he took the roll and pulled it back over the wing and the bullet's exit hole. He jumped off the barrel, went under the wing, and did the same thing two more times until there was a continuous patch from the bottom, around the front, to the top of the wing.

Eventually, the roll of tape became a big silver stripe on the blue wing like a racing stripe.

"Cool." He closed his eyes and whispered a quick prayer. "Father, keep Your hand on this tape and let it hold so I can get Geesler back to Bishop."

Facing the wind, the plane taxied out onto the road. It seemed to have little power to fight the gusts as it rolled down the roadway. Then it leaped into the air, rocking against the gales.

The patch job was holding ... for now. The airplane climbed fast; air speed was a hundred miles per hour. Making it before dark was highly doubtful.

The flight back to Geesler was still a long way. It was late as the sun hung low in the sky.

When Bishop finally came in to view, Josh circled around and landed on the cross-runway. Jerry Austin walked out of the lower building as Josh taxied up to the tower.

"Hey, young Powers. How did you wreck your plane or is that a silver racing stripe?"

"I had a little trouble."

Josh decided this wasn't the time to bring up Al-Razi who was stuck out on an abandon runway, away from the highway, in a sand storm, with an empty gun. Hopefully he found shelter somewhere.

"Mr. Austin, I really need to get back to Emerson Lake and pick up Dr. Geesler. He's the father of the girl I brought in."

"What's the speed tape on your airplane for?" Austin ran his hand over the tape.

"Hole was poked through the wing." Josh shrugged. He saw no need to mention the bullet.

"You say you're going back out to Emerson Lake? What were you doing down south?"

"Had to take a friend down there."

"Okay. I see. Well, young Powers, I don't think I'd fly the plane with tape on the wing. Why don't you let me fix it tonight and you can leave tomorrow? Is it a big hole?"

"Mr. Austin, I really have to go tonight. Mr. Geesler needs to be with his daughter."

"If I let you go and the wing fails over the dry lake, I would feel guilty."

"I know but I need to pick up Mr. Geesler."

Jerry Austin shook his head. "If you feel that strong about it, let me fill your airplane with gas. One less thing to think about, right?"

"Right. Thank you." Josh watched Austin fill the gas tank, but his thoughts turned to Al-Razi—would he carry out his mission? It was real and dangerous.

Homeland Security should be told or at least the local police. That settled it. Josh decided to come clean and let Austin know the truth. He began with the conflict between Al-Razi and Geesler; Al-Razi's relationship with Brenda; Al-Razi's gun; and Al-Razi's mission.

"Where is this Al-Razi fella now?"

"Stuck in a windstorm. He wanted me to fly him to LAX, but I told him we couldn't go there even in an emergency. On our way there, a storm came. Al-Razi was pretty scared and wanted out of the plane."

"Where did you let him out? Lone Pine?"

"No. Manzanar. Al-Razi jumped out as soon as we landed. I took that as my chance to escape so I put the power in and took off."

"Did he shoot at you? Is that how you got the hole in your wing?"

"Yes." Josh whispered. "It creased the tank, but didn't punch a hole in it."

"Where did you get the chance to make the repairs?"

"I landed on a dirt road by some old truck scales."

Austin topped off the tanks. "You're a lucky man, young Powers. Very lucky."

"I know. Thanks for the gas. I'm sure my dad will pay you for it."

"No need. Hopefully he won't be mad at me for letting you fly off in a shot-up airplane." Jerry Austin walked to the right-side window as Josh got into the plane.

"Godspeed, young Powers." Austin reached in and patted his shoulder. "Keep your eye on that patch. If it goes bad, put the plane on the ground. If you're not back in a couple of days, I'll be out lookin' for you."

Josh nodded, pushed the throttle forward, and taxied out to the runway. He had forty-five minutes to an hour flight ahead of him. Sunlight was fading. It would be impossible to land on a lakebed without lights.

Chapter 8

The sun had gone down behind the Sierra Nevada Mountains. Josh let his Piper PA-11 climb as high as it could. Weather conditions were tough and the plane bounced along. At eight thousand feet he hoped it would smooth out.

He looked out the side windows, paying attention to the high mountains looming on either side. Josh followed the glimmer of headlights from the cars below.

The tailwind shortened the trip back to the lake. Yet daylight was dim now and Josh strained his eyes to locate a nearby tunnel. To make matters worse, as he flew round a corner, the glimmer of headlights disappeared. *The cars must have gone into the tunnel.* Josh's body tensed but he kept a steady flight path to the right.

A car suddenly appeared from the tunnel providing the much-needed light. At least he knew where the tunnel was and could adjust his flight path accordingly.

Three more cars drove out of the tunnel as Josh passed the opening. He maneuvered the air-plane over the highway and flew straight toward the white, dry lakebed.

By this time, the moon was only a sliver but enough of its light reflected onto the lakebed. The flags on the end of the runway, however, were in-visible.

Josh left the throttle where it was and pushed the nose of the plane down. He set up a glideslope which would take him to the other side of the dry lake and the runway.

Wind screamed passed the windows. He checked his airspeed. About twenty more minutes and he would have to land. The storm grew worse. *Maybe landing elsewhere would be safer*, he thought. He checked his watch; ten minutes to go.

Leaning forward Josh pushed a little harder on the stick. The plane plummeted with its landing lights shining directly onto the ground. He pulled up, leveling off until the plane slowed. And then he saw it: In the distance, off to the right, a small glow flickered from what looked like a camp-fire.

A second fire burned about a width of the runway away. "Geesler!" *Who else would be out here?* Josh thought. *That has to be Geesler.*

Josh headed for the new markers. A small beam of light waved around in the air. "Thank you Lord, and thank you, Mr. Geesler."

As Josh landed close to the fires, Easton Geesler walked out of the dark. Josh pushed the side window open.

Geesler stuck his head into the cockpit. "Joshua. How are you, Lad? And where is Al-Razi?"

"It's a long story, which I'll tell you later."

Geesler nodded. "All right then. I'm glad you saw the light. We are out on the end of the runway. Let me get in and we'll taxi to the other end. It's a half mile up to the terminal with the wooden bench. I have two buckets of cement on the other side of the bench." Geesler waved his arm to the right. "You can park in between them."

Josh made his way to the back side of the bench and parked the plane between the two buckets of cement and cut the engine.

When the winds died down and millions of stars appeared in the sky, Josh told Geesler all the happenings of the day. Then the young pilot let out a sigh and gave thanks. "Thank You, Father, for Your protection and for all the wonders of Your creation."

"Yes. Yes. Thank You for the mighty works of Your hand." Geesler raised his hands toward heaven. "Do you know, Joshua, that the Bible says God placed all the stars in the sky and gave each one a name? Every single one of them."

Josh was stargazing. "It kinda makes you feel small, doesn't it?"

"It does indeed. God, the creator of the universe, came to this earth, and He even knows our names. That is how personal He is."

"I told Al-Razi that God knew his name." Josh squinted into the night air. "But why would a big and mighty God take an interest in someone like him ... or me?"

"Because, God's love is unconditional."

"Maybe Al-Razi will see that too someday."

"Well, Joshua, we better get this plane tied down. You never know if the wind will pick up again during the night. You probably want to stay here for the night. That pass would be treacherous to fly through."

"It was pretty scary alright," Josh said. "By the way where did you find these buckets? I didn't see them last I was here."

"They were behind the shack up the trail. I was too stressed and confused to remember."

"How did you know to light these fires?" Josh picked up a rope to tie the plane to the bucket of cement.

"That's an old SAS trick. During the war I flew spies into France. The Parisians would line cans of petrol for us so we could land. Of course, they were square petrol cans with one side cut out so the Germans couldn't see them from the side or back. You could only see them burning from one side."

"How did you know I was coming?"

"I just knew. As it got darker I took these two pans and filled them with petrol from Roy's truck. When I heard your plane and saw the landing light, I touched them off."

Josh looked again for something to chock the wheels. He found a big rock, but when he re-turned both wheels had professionally made chock blocks holding them in place.

"Where did these come from?"

"They were piled behind that bush." Geesler pointed off into the dark.

"Do you have many guests out here with airplanes?"

"Oh yes. I have people fly out from all over the country to have a silent prayer retreat. Important people."

"Where do they stay?"

"I let them stay in my cabin. The desert silence and solitude is what they are after."

"Where do you stay when they're here?"

"I stay in the shack where the miners used to keep the explosives. You and I can spend the night there. It is fixed up quite nicely."

When they got to the miner's shack, Geesler lit a kerosene lamp. The bunk beds, built out of two-by-fours, had wooden boards on the bottom but no mattresses. An old, tattered, green army blanket lay neatly folded on the end of each bed.

"Joshua, you can take the top bunk bed."

Josh lay down on the hard wooden boards and covered himself. The desert grew cold during the night as wind rushed through a hole just above Joshua's head. He pulled the blanket up, wrapped it around his head, and fell asleep from sheer exhaustion.

The next morning, the sun hit him right in the eye, causing temporary blindness. Plus, he was sore and cold. Josh wrapped the blanket tighter around his body and breathed warmth into it.

"Good morning, Joshua," came a cheery voice from beneath him. "How did you sleep, my boy?"

"Not very well."

"I slept splendidly. I'm glad you're awake. We need to get going so I can get to the hospital to see Brenda. All I could do was pray for her."

Josh moaned, swung his legs over the edge of the bed, and sat up. "What time is it?"

"It's about 6:15, I suspect."

Josh yawned, scratched his head and rub-bed his eyes. Once on the ground, he continued to yawn and stretched. "Do you have anything to eat?"

"We will eat when we get to Bishop. Let's inspect the plane, shall we?"

Still half asleep Josh examined the patch on the wing. Carefully he slid his hand along the tape on the bottom of the wing and traced it to the top as far as he could reach. Everything seemed to be in place.

"How long will it take us to get to Bishop, Joshua?" Geesler squeezed into the back seat.

Josh checked the controls and did his magneto check. "It should only take about forty-five minutes to an hour." He advanced the throttle, and turned onto the runway. The airplane rolled into the still, morning air. Josh kept a steady pressure on the stick as the plane climbed to altitude.

"God, thank You for this beautiful day. Please let us get to Brenda in one piece. Amen," Josh whispered. "Mr. Geesler, do you know much about snakes and their bites?"

"Not really. I know it damages the muscle. Every snake in the world affects you in a different way. It's the most powerful poison of all animals."

"I sure hope Brenda is okay."

"Yes, as do I. We will know soon enough."

Josh glanced over his shoulder at Geesler who tried to fight back the tears. The old man stared out the side widow and sat that way for the rest of the trip.

When they got through the pass, Josh radioed Bishop Unicom. "Bishop Unicom. This is Piper 2-3 Juliet Papa. Over." He waited for a response. "Bishop Unicom. This is Piper 2-3 Juliet Papa. Over." He called three more times before someone answered.

"Piper 2-3 Juliet Papa. Is that you, young Powers?"

"Yes sir, Mr. Austin. Over."

"What do you need, Son?"

"Mr. Austin, I have Mr. Geesler with me.

The girl's father. Could you call a taxi for us so we can get to the hospital?"

"I can do that. Need anything else?"

"I'm coming straight on the cross-runway, if

that's okay?"

"That'll be fine. We don't have any reported traffic this morning. It's early yet."

Josh loved to fly in the morning air. The plane glided through the blue sky and gave him a sense of peace. On the final approach, he radioed one more time. "Bishop Unicom. This is Piper 2-3 Juliet Papa on a straight in final on runaway two-zero. Over."

"Roger that, 2-3 Juliet Papa. Over."

The plane floated down to the ground; tires squealing on the asphalt—a good landing.

"That was a passenger landing, Joshua. I'd fly anywhere with you," Geesler said.

"Thank you, Mr. Geesler."

Jerry Austin walked out of his office at the bottom of the building. "Go ahead and park there!" Austin pointed out directions.

Josh taxied the plane and stopped over the cable, which ran across the ground. Mr. Austin walked up and chocked both front wheels while Josh cut the engine.

"Did you call us a cab, Mr. Austin?" Josh picked up one of the ropes tied to a cable and connected the loose end to the tie-down ring under
the wing.

"No. I decided to take you up there myself." Jerry Austin tied the other wing. "I've got a new pickup. This will give me a chance to drive it."

"That would be nice of you," Geesler said. My daughter is in the hospital, you know, and we would like to get up there as soon as possible."

"I saw her when Josh brought her in. She didn't look too good. I'm sure she's all right now though," Austin said.

"I hope and pray she is." Geesler sighed and shook his head.

When they pulled into the hospital parking lot, Geesler jumped out and hobbled as fast as he could into the lobby.

"Mr. Austin, thank you so much. You have been a big help. I will repay, I promise." Josh slapped the side of Austin's truck. "Mr. Geesler is in a hurry to see his daughter. He is really worried about her."

"I know young Powers. I would be worried too, if it were my daughter in there. Listen, if you need anything, anything at all, give me a call. I would be glad to give you a hand. When you get ready to leave, I'll take you back to the airport." Austin gave a short salute. "Oh, by the way, I called the police and Homeland Security on your guy, Roy Al-Razi. Hope you don't mind."

"No, I don't mind at all. Thank you."

Chapter 9

Josh rushed into the hospital and found Geesler asking for directions from the person behind the desk.

"Room 334B. Go to the elevators and up to the third floor. It's on your right."

"Thank you, Miss." Geesler headed for the elevator.

Josh followed but stopped for a moment. A man sitting in the waiting room peeked over the top of a newspaper. He was clean shaven, with short black hair, and his sunglasses hid his eyes. There was something very familiar about him, but Josh couldn't place him. It was unsettling, but for now his only concern was Brenda.

"Joshua, are you coming?" Geesler held the elevator door ajar.

Josh smiled and hustled inside.

As the elevator came to a stop and the door opened, Geesler walked off in the wrong direction.

"Mr. Geesler, I think it's this way."

"Yes. Oh yes." Geesler turned around and proceeded toward the nurses' station. "I am Geesler.

Dr. Easton Geesler, Brenda's father. I would like to see my daughter, please."

"She's down the hall in 334, bed B. Doctor Randall is with her right now. He would like to talk to you." The nurse led them to the room. "Doctor Randall. This is Brenda's father."

"Easton Geesler. Nice to meet you, Doctor." Geesler held out his hand.

"Mr. Geesler, it's nice to meet you," said Dr. Randall. "Brenda is doing fine. We gave her an anti-venom shot and the swelling is going down. She'll be sore for a while, but like I said, she's doing fine. We have to operate to remove the dead tissue, then we'll know better." The doctor gently shook Brenda out of her sleep. "Brenda, your dad is here to see you."

Brenda opened her sleepy eyes. "Hi Daddy."

Geesler's eyes widened. She hadn't called him Daddy for years. "Hello angel. How are you doing? Joshua is here to see you too."

Josh moved closer to her bed. "Hi Brenda, I'm glad the swelling is going down. You and your dad probably need a few minutes alone. I'll go get something to eat."

Brenda reached out and touched his arm. "Thank you, Josh, for everything."

Josh nodded and together with Dr. Randall headed for the door.

Dr. Randall, with one hand on the door knob, turned to Geesler. "I'll get someone to look at your head-wound."

Josh found the cafeteria and ordered a sandwich. He was about to say grace when he felt a hand on his shoulder and a familiar voice sneering at him.

"You thought you could leave me in the desert."

The grip on his shoulder tightened. Josh jumped. "Al-Razi?"

Al-Razi took off his sunglasses, showed off his clean-shaven face, and unbuttoned his blue shirt. "You can't ditch your old friend Roy that easy." He had his hand on the handle of a pistol, which was partially hidden beneath his shirt. "Get up, we're out of here."

Josh glanced around the room. Everyone was busy eating lunch or talking with friends. For some reason he grabbed half his sandwich.

"Drop the sandwich. You should suffer like I did."

A security guard walked in to the cafeteria and stepped in line.

Al-Razi poked Josh sharply in the ribs with the barrel of a gun. "Don't say a word. Walk slowly toward the exit."

As they approached the nurse at the front desk, she stood. "Did you get to see that poor girl?"

"Yes, I did," Josh replied.

Al-Razi jabbed him in the ribs again.

"Oh good. I'm glad. You have a nice day," the nurse said.

"We will," Al-Razi said.

In the parking lot, for a fleeting moment, Josh thought about escaping. He didn't think Al-Razi had any bullets left. But maybe he had bought some. Maybe he found some in the mineshaft? Josh couldn't take the chance.

"Go there." Al-Razi pointed to a gray pick-up. He pushed Josh toward it, opened the door, and shoved him inside.

Al-Razi reached inside his pocket and pulled out two wire ties. He placed one tie around Josh's wrist, and cinched it up tight; then slipped the other tie under the first one and clamped it to his other wrist.

"Get on the floor!" Al-Razi looked around the parking lot. "I don't want you to make eye contact with anyone."

Josh slid off the seat.

Al-Razi slammed the door. "That's better." He shoved a screw-driver into the spot where the ignition switch had been.

Josh bowed his head and prayed silently. *Father, please help me to find favor with Al-Razi. Give me courage. Amen.*

"Praying to your God again?" Al-Razi's voice was filled with sarcasm as he drove out of the parking lot and into the flow of traffic.

"Yes, I was."

"He never answers. He never says anything. I have thoughts of my own and I don't need any interference from Him."

"Well, the Bible says God works all things for good to those who love Him. That's all I was asking Him."

"So you think He's going to turn everything to sunshine and little white flowers. He's never met me."

"Oh, God has met you. God knows you, Roy. He knows everything about you. And, believe it or not, he even loved you enough to send His Son to die for you."

Al-Razi checked the rearview mirror, ignoring the conversation. Twenty minutes later he turned onto an old track in the desert. Dust filtered into the truck, making Josh sick.

The young pilot coughed and doubled over. "I think I'm going to throw up."

"Good. I want you to be miserable."

"You won't think it's good when I puke on you."

Al-Razi slammed on the brakes and jumped out. He flung the door open. "Get out! Get out, now!"

Josh straightened up and made his way to a large boulder. Fresh air helped the nausea pass.

Al-Razi ordered him to get back in the truck. "Just sit up!" he shouted. "Nobody will see you out here."

Josh got in the front seat of the truck and tried to get comfortable. "What are you going to do with me?"

You will see soon enough. You better keep praying."

The truck rolled till it stopped beside an old cabin with a picket fence and a flagstone pathway.

Al-Razi backed up to the side of the cabin and opened the truck door. "Get out!"

Josh stumbled out and headed for the front door of the cabin.

"Not that way. Out back."

In the back corner of the yard stood a shack with its door kicked in. The lock and frame were broken and splintered.

Al-Razi pulled out his gun. "You will not be going into the cabin. Get in the shed."

Josh nodded, pushed open the door with his foot and walked into the shed.

Al-Razi continued with his barrage of orders. "Get on your knees facing the back of the room."

Josh knelt. His heart pounding. Would Al-Razi shoot him? He closed his eyes.

"You can stay right there ... in that position, while I decide what to do with you. You do not get to move. I will be able to watch you from the cabin." Al-Razi backed out of the storage shed, leaving the door propped open.

For two hours Josh stayed on his knees. When he finally heard the back door of the cabin squeak open he prayed. "Dear Father, give me courage; control my fear. No matter what Al-Razi does give me the strength to overcome it. Amen."

"Joshua." Al-Razi paced the floor. "I've done some dumb things in my life. But the dumbest was kidnapping you. Please forgive me." He clenched his fists and breathed short, shallow breaths.

"What did you say?" Josh was at a loss for words, and not sure if he believed it.

"Can you forgive me." Al-Razi hung his head. "After you left me behind in that abandoned airport, I sat in the cold, dusty wind all night." He wiped his forehead which only managed to spread the dirt. "I wanted to get even with you. But it made me think of everything my father had told me over the years: how much God loves me. You know, all that stuff you said. God loves me. God knows me."

"Yeah well ... God does love us." Josh sighed and shook his head. "In spite of all the dumb things we've done."

"I know. I messed up. I asked God to forgive me."

"You did?" Josh took a little while to think. "Okay, does this mean you're going to take these things off my wrists?" Josh turned his shoulders. "And hopefully this means you're not going to shoot me?"

"I did not even have any bullets left. I emptied my gun when I shot at your plane." Al-Razi raised his eyebrows. "Did I hit it?"

"You did a little damage, but I survived."

Al-Razi found wire cutters on a workbench and cut Josh's ties. The young pilot sat on the floor stretching out his arms and legs. He moaned as he rubbed his wrists and cracked his back.

Al-Razi squatted beside him. A few tears began to fall, but Josh looked away.

"I am sorry I did this to you." Al-Razi put the wire cutters back on the bench. "I was cold, alone, and really hungry. I did not know where I was; feeling nauseated from that horrible flight through the hurricane-like winds and then I remembered what you said to me. 'God will take care of you.' I guess I am like the prodigal son. Actually, I tried not to think about it, but there I was. My father had taught me the truth ... I knew the truth, but I did not want to accept it. I had a lot of things to work out."

Josh sat quietly, listening, surprised by how much Al-Razi knew about God.

"You really did get to me, Josh. I have always known that God had a plan for me but I guess I never felt it until I spent a night on my own in the desert ... alone and hurt, mind you."

For a while they both sat silently. Josh didn't know what to say. He squeezed his head between his knees.

"Joshua, let us go back to town. I have some things I must take care of and then I am going to turn myself in."

Though he had his doubts about Al-Razi's turnabout, he agreed and shook on it.

When they arrived at the hospital, police officers were stationed around the lobby. A few officers walked up to Josh and looked him over.

"Are you Joshua Powers?" one of them asked. "Are you all right?"

"Yes, I'm Joshua Powers."

"What's this about a guy named Roy Al-Razi? Do you know where he is?"

"Yes, he's right ..." Josh turned around and realized Al-Razi was no longer with him. *Oh no*, he thought. *I should've known.* He covered his eyes with his fingertips. "I'm sorry, Officer, I don't know where he went. He came to turn himself in. He must have changed his mind and slipped off somewhere."

One of the police officers ran outside. "I'll take a look."

"We hear he has a terrorist plot in mind," said another officer.

"Yeah, he said he had a mission to carry out at LAX. He was going to blow something up. You'll have to talk to him about it."

"We will ... when we get him. Don't go anywhere. Why don't you visit your friend, maybe he'll show up there."

Josh took the elevator up to the third floor and walked down the hall to Brenda's room. He was puzzled and shook his head continually.

"Joshua! Where did you go? I looked all over for you." Geesler stood up and put his hand on Josh's shoulder. "I even called the police."

Josh sighed. "Roy is back."

Chapter 10

The news of Al-Razi's return did not sit well with Brenda and Geesler.

"Al-Razi is back?" Geesler breathed into his cupped hands.

"Where is he?" Brenda sat up in bed and looked around. "I have something I need to tell him."

Josh shrugged his shoulders. "He was coming back here to confess. I should've known better when he got a wild look in his eyes. And he was mumbling something I couldn't understand."

"Oh, I wish he would just leave us alone. He's got a nasty temper." Geesler ruffled his hair.

Josh examined Brenda's leg. "It doesn't look like the swelling has gone down much at all. It still seems discolored."

"They're going to have to operate, remove the dead skin, and replace it with a skin graft." Brenda covered her leg with the bed sheets, feeling a little uncomfortable with Josh staring at it.

"Is it painful?" Josh asked.

"For a time I thought I was going to die. It doesn't hurt as much today. It sure is ugly though."

"It'll be all right." Josh tried to be positive for her.

"Dr. Randall says I'll have a scar, which will need plastic surgery. But if they can't make it look good, I'll just wear pants and cover it up."

In the middle of their conversation, Josh heard the door close. He held up his hand. His heart skipped a few beats. Suddenly, the curtain drawn around Brenda's bed ripped apart, revealing Al-Razi holding a pair of scissors. Josh's mouth dropped wide open. Both Brenda and Josh held their breaths.

Geesler stood up and stepped toward him. "Roy, you are not welcome here. Please leave."

Roy pointed the scissors at Geesler's face. "You are the one who caused all of my problems! You lied to me. You never had the Sword!"

The back of Josh's neck tingled. His voice shook. "What happened to you Roy? Didn't you ask God to forgive you? Was that a lie?"

"Do not worry, Powers. God forgave me for what I did to you, and He's about to forgive me for what I am going to do to this old man." Al-Razi closed the gap between Geesler and himself.

"Roy! Shut up and listen." Brenda tried to make eye contact. "I have something I need to tell you."

"*You* shut up and listen. I have something I need to tell you." Roy's breaths were shallow and his eyes narrowed. "I was trying to get the Sword from your lying father. I never loved you. You never did anything I told you. You are a shameful and weak woman."

Tears rolled down Brenda's cheeks, shocked by his harsh words. But Roy continued his tirade even when Dr. Randall walked into the room.

The doctor froze on the spot and let the door close behind him. "Um, excuse me. We need to get Brenda to the O.R. asap." He tried his best to ignore Al-Razi. "We can go right now."

"That would be splendid." Easton Geesler edged toward the door.

"You are not going anywhere, old man, except with me."

Geesler backed up as frightened hospital staff came into the room.

"Get her out of here!" Al-Razi waved the scissors like a sword.

The staff hurriedly folded the sagging blankets and wheeled Brenda out of the room.

Brenda reached for Al-Razi's hand as she passed by. "Roy, I forgive you. But please don't hurt my dad."

"I do not need your forgiveness." Al-Razi grabbed Geesler from behind. They stumbled toward Josh. With a quick and violent motion Al-Razi wrapped his other arm around Josh's neck.

"Mr. Al-Razi!" Doctor Randal pled his case. "Mr. Geesler is an old man. He would like to see his daughter have this surgery. Maybe you could let him go for now."

"Do I look stupid to you? Get over by the window! Down on your knees!"

Doctor Randall did what he was told. He turned slowly and faced the window.

Al-Razi pushed his captives to the door, tightening his grip around Geesler's chest. The scissors poking Geesler's throat. He let go of the stranglehold on Josh for a moment to open the door. But out in the hall, Al-Razi came face to face with a large number of police—guns drawn and pointing at him.

"Get on the ground! On the ground, now!"

Al-Razi froze for five seconds, then grabbed Geesler by the hair and cut the skin on the surface of his throat. "Get back, all of you! Get back or I'll cut him deeper!"

Blood trickled down Geesler's neck. He went limp. Al-Razi tightened his arm around Josh's neck.

A police negotiator behind Al-Razi calmly spoke. "We don't have to do it this way."

Al-Razi spun both of his captives around, getting more agitated by the minute. "Get back! I will hurt them."

"Why don't you put the scissors down and let's talk about this."

"I have a better idea. Back off!"

"Okay, okay." The negotiator raised his hands. "We can do that."

The police officers backed up with their guns still pointing at Al-Razi. They all shuffled down the corridor.

"That's good, Mr. Al-Razi. Let's keep it going slow."

Al-Razi turned and ran.

One police officer burst through the door. "Get the doctor!"

Someone hurried down the hall to get Dr. Randall.

"Which way did he go?" an officer asked.

Geesler pointed westward. "I believe he went that way."

Josh gently moved Geesler off his chest and kneeled beside him. "I'm sorry Mr. Geesler. I never should've let him come back. I thought he had changed."

Dr. Randall rushed through the door and examined Geesler. "Get this man to the ER, fast!"

Orderlies hoisted Geesler onto a gurney and wheeled him away. It was chaos as police ran around them.

"Are you all right, young man?" Dr. Randall put his hand on Josh's shoulder.

"Yeah ... I think so."

One of the officers came back holding the pair of scissors with two fingers. "Found the weapon." He placed them in an evidence bag. "Do you have any idea where he would go or who he would go see?"

Josh shook his head. "He told me he was coming here to surrender. Something changed his mind. He's a very angry man."

"We have men all around the building and grounds looking for him. He won't get away. We know what he looks like now."

Two officers were assigned to Josh to keep him safe. Police checked everyone as they left the hospital, the grounds were searched as well as every car and truck.

Josh returned to the front desk and asked about Geesler's condition.

"He's resting comfortably in his daughter's room." The nurse checked her paperwork.

A guard was posted outside of the room.

"Can I see Mr. Geesler?"

"Name?"

"Joshua Powers."

The guard pulled out a paper and checked the short list of names. He ran his finger down the page. "Ah, here you are. Go on in."

Josh cracked the door open and peeked inside. "Mr. Geesler? It's Joshua."

Geesler stirred. A white bandage wrapped around his neck. "Joshua? How nice to see you safe. Have they caught that rascal yet?"

"I'm not sure. But no need to worry. There's a guard outside the door."

"Good. Very good indeed. Have you heard anything about Brenda?"

"We can call the nurse and ask her." Josh pushed the call button on the side of the bed.

"How can I help you?"

"Do you know anything about ..." Geesler crunched his eyebrows and scratched his head.

"Mr. Geesler wants to know how Brenda's surgery is going," Joshua said.

"I will check and get back to you."

Josh put his hand on Geesler's arm. "How bad was the cut?"

"Not so bad. It was only a small puncture. I'm just tired."

Josh stood silent for about five minutes, then sat down holding on to Geesler's hand. "How can a man like Al-Razi, ask for forgiveness and talk about being a prodigal son, then continue life as if nothing's changed?"

"That's a good question, Joshua. There are people who always look for a fire escape in life. They think God will notice if they say the right words and do the right things. But they continue to do what they want." Geesler squeezed Joshua's hand. "Dear lad, Al-Razi is a wicked man. His heart was bent on destruction and you were not the problem. I wasn't either, but he sure directed his anger toward us."

Geesler's nurse walked into the room with a smile. "How are you doing, Mr. Geesler?"

"I'm fine, young lady. Have you learned anything about my daughter's surgery?"

"Yes, Brenda did just fine in surgery. She's in recovery and will be back in her room within an hour."

"Splendid."

"If you need anything, let me know."

Josh closed the door as the nurse walked back to her desk. "Mr. Geesler, do you think Al-Razi loves God?"

"Joshua, he's in such a confused state of mind. He has politics mixed up with two religions. We need to keep praying for him."

"I can do that."

Geesler nodded and closed his eyes.

Josh whispered, "I'll check back in an hour. Get some rest."

Josh breathed in the fresh air as he walked outside. Police were still searching for Al-Razi. Thank You, God, for protecting us today."

Loud shouts of, "Get on the ground! Get on the ground," interrupted his thoughts. He ran to the corner, toward the bedlam. Three police officers had wrestled Al-Razi to the ground.

"Stop resisting. You're gonna get hurt."

Al-Razi fought their every move. A fourth officer jumped on top of the pile and handcuffed him. But when the officer stood up, Al-Razi kicked his leg and knocked him down. Two more officers came and the wrestling match continued.

Finally, they restrained him with a leather strap, which they tied around his neck to his ankles.

"Others will come. They will blow up your airports!" Al-Razi's face turned red, saliva spewed out of his mouth.

At that point a spit bag was thrown over his head. But Al-Razi continued to swear in the officers' faces. "Prison will be a blessing because there are no cowards in prison. The Brotherhood will protect me!"

"What a piece of work." One officer shook his head and turned to Josh. "You're lucky to be alive."

"No, officer, it's not luck at all. Unlike Al-Razi's brotherhood, my God protects me, rescues me, and he's concerned about me." He shook the officer's hand. And with a smile, Joshua Powers was able to walk away from the chaos of the day.

Made in the USA
San Bernardino, CA
08 March 2020